Christmas at Grandma's House

Christmas at Grandma's House

Written and Illustrated by P. K. Hallinan

ideals children's books.
Nashville, Tennessee

ISBN-13: 978-0-8249-5535-9
ISBN-10: 0-8249-5535-8

Published by Ideals Children's Books
An imprint of Ideals Publications
A Guideposts Company
535 Metroplex Drive, Suite 250
Nashville, Tennessee 37211
www.idealsbooks.com

Color separations by Precision Color Graphics, Franklin, Wisconsin

Printed and bound in Italy by LEGO

Library of Congress Cataloging-in-Publication Data

Hallinan, P. K.
    Christmas at Grandma's house / P.K. Hallinan.
        p. cm.
    Summary: Rhyming text describes the joys of spending Christmas day at Grandma's house, opening gifts, eating dinner, and sharing stories.
    ISBN 0-8249-5535-8 (alk. paper)
    [1. Christmas—Fiction. 2. Grandmothers—Fiction. 3. Stories in rhyme.]   I. Title.
PZ8.3.H15Ch 2006
[E]—dc22
                                        2006011579

10 9 8 7 6 5 4 3 2

Designed by Georgina Chidlow-Rucker

This Book
Belongs to

_____

When the gifts are all opened,
And the stockings emptied too,
We still have one wonderful
Thing left to do!

It's Christmas at Grandma's,
Where the whole family meets
For a day full of laughter
And holiday treats!

Now with time running late,
We can hardly wait!

We run to our rooms
And quickly get dressed.

We shine up our faces
So we're looking our best!

Then we hop in the car,
Put our seat belts in place,
And drive down the street
At a leisurely pace.

And we sing Christmas songs
As we jingle along.

The world seems so quiet
As we travel our way.
There are very few cars
On the highway today.

And we hold Grandma's presents
On our laps, good and tight,
As we gaze at the haze
In the late-morning light.

By the roadside, two crows
Peck at patches of snow.

Sometimes we'll stop
For a light little snack.
Or sometimes we'll stop
To just stretch and relax.

But we're quick to move on,
Without any fuss,
Because getting to Grandma's
Is important to us.

So we sit back and wait,
Counting out-of-state plates.

Then suddenly, we're there!
Our hearts beat so fast!
We've arrived in the driveway
Of Grandma's house at last!

Grandma stands in the doorway,
With her wonderful smile,
To meet us and greet us
In her holiday style!

Then we joyfully race
To her loving embrace!

Inside, there's the fragrance
Of turkey and cider.
Aunt Jenny is there—
Uncle Bill's right beside her.

And our cousins are waiting,
With patience and glee,
To open the presents
That garnish the tree.

And Grandma's warm grin
Says it's time to begin.

Each present is opened
With delight and surprise!
Then Grandma opens hers
With some breathless "Oh my's!"

And everyone laughs
Because Grandma always frets,
And says, "It's too expensive!"
No matter what she gets.

But what can we say?
She's thoughtful that way.

Soon we move on
To the big Christmas meal,
Where the turkey's revealed
Amid clapping and squeals.

Then we all join our hands
As we say a short prayer
For the food Grandma's cooked
And for folks everywhere.

Then everyone smiles
and digs in for a while.

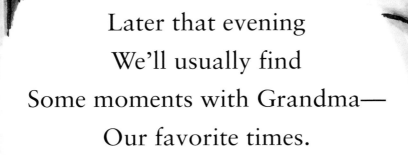

Later that evening
We'll usually find
Some moments with Grandma—
Our favorite times.

Amid all the clamor
And the holiday fuss,
She's never too busy
To make room for us.

And she listens with care
To the words that we share.

It's always unclear
How this holiday ends—
We usually wake up
In the car once again.

And we sleepily say,
As we gaze at the lights,
That Grandma makes Christmas
So happy and bright.

And there's really no doubt
She's one of a kind . . .

Yes, Christmas at Grandma's
Is a wonderful time!